HALI SIMMONS

Loving A Monster

Copyright © 2025 by Hali Simmons

All rights reserved. No part of this publication may be reproduced, stored or transmitted in any form or by any means, electronic, mechanical, photocopying, recording, scanning, or otherwise without written permission from the publisher. It is illegal to copy this book, post it to a website, or distribute it by any other means without permission.

This novel is entirely a work of fiction. The names, characters and incidents portrayed in it are the work of the author's imagination. Any resemblance to actual persons, living or dead, events or localities is entirely coincidental.

Hali Simmons asserts the moral right to be identified as the author of this work.

Hali Simmons has no responsibility for the persistence or accuracy of URLs for external or third-party Internet Websites referred to in this publication and does not guarantee that any content on such Websites is, or will remain, accurate or appropriate.

Designations used by companies to distinguish their products are often claimed as trademarks. All brand names and product names used in this book and on its cover are trade names, service marks, trademarks and registered trademarks of their respective owners. The publishers and the book are not associated with any product or vendor mentioned in this book. None of the companies referenced within the book have endorsed the book.

First edition

*This book was professionally typeset on Reedsy.
Find out more at reedsy.com*

Contents

1	Eyes Like a Blade	1
2	Alianne	2
3	Maddox	5
4	Dark Fascination	7
5	Alianne	8
6	Maddox	10
7	Maddox	12
8	Alianne	14
9	Maddox	16
10	Alianne	18
11	Maddox	20
12	Alianne	21
13	Alianne	22
14	Chase Me, Break Me	24
15	Maddox	25
16	Alianne	26
17	Maddox	27
18	Alianne	29
19	Maddox	31
20	Alianne	32
21	Maddox	33
22	Alianne	34
23	Maddox	36
24	Alianne	38

25	Maddox	40
26	Alianne	42
27	Maddox	43
28	Alianne	44
29	Maddox	46
30	Maddox	48
31	Alianne	50
32	Maddox	51
33	Alianne	53
34	Maddox	55
35	Maddox	56
36	Alianne	58
37	Maddox	59
38	Alianne	61
39	Maddox	62
40	Alianne	64
41	Maddox	65
42	Alianne	67
43	Alianne	68
44	Maddox	70
45	Alianne	71
46	Maddox	72
47	Alianne	73
48	Alianne	75
49	Maddox	77
50	Alianne	79
51	Maddox	81
52	Alianne	82
53	Maddox	83
54	Claimed in Dirt and Sky	85
55	Alianne	87

56	Maddox	88
57	Alianne	89
58	Alianne	90
59	Maddox	92
60	Alianne	94
61	Maddox	95
62	Alianne	96
63	Maddox	97
64	Alianne	98
65	Maddox	99
66	Tangled in Filth and Worship	100
67	Maddox	102
68	Alianne	104
69	Maddox	105
70	Maddox	107
71	Maddox	109
72	Maddox	110
73	Alianne	111
74	Maddox	112
75	Maddox	113
76	Alianne	114
77	Alianne	115
78	Maddox	117
79	Alianne	118
80	Maddox	119
81	Alianne	120
82	Alianne	122
83	Alianne	124
84	Maddox	126
85	Maddox	127
86	Alianne	128

87	Maddox	129
88	Alianne	130
89	Maddox	131
90	Maddox	132
91	Alianne	133
92	Alianne	134
93	The Price of Smiling	135
94	Maddox	136
95	Alianne	138
96	Maddox	139
97	Alianne	140
98	Alianne	141
99	Wrong Hands, Wrong Love	142
100	Alianne	143
101	Alianne	145
102	Alianne	146
103	Bleed Me, Leave Me	147
104	Alianne	148
105	Maddox	150
106	Maddox	151
107	Maddox	152
108	Maddox	154
109	Maddox	156
110	Maddox	159
111	Maddox	160
112	A Vow Written in Blood	162
113	Alianne	163
114	Maddox	165
115	Alianne	167
116	Worship the Wreckage	168
117	Maddox	169

118	Alianne	170
119	Maddox	171
120	No God But You	172
121	Maddox	173

One

Eyes Like a Blade

Your stare was a blade.

Sharp as a vow.

cutting through crowds.

To find me somehow.

I wasn't ready.

I wasn't warned.

I still stepped closer.

I still got torn.

Two

Alianne

My hands wouldn't stop fidgeting.

Twisting the strap of my backpack.

Smoothing my skirt.

Pushing up my glasses.

Over and over again.

I hated new places.

I hated feeling watched.

And today, I was drowning in it.

Alianne

The lecture hall buzzed with noise.

Laughing, flirting, the snap of gum and notebooks.

But all I could focus on was how alone I felt.

I made it three steps into the room before I tripped.

My books crashed to the floor in a humiliating, thunderous avalanche.

But he did.

He stood against the far wall.

Lazy, predatory king of the ruins.

Black jeans, white T-shirt stretched across a broad chest.

Dark hair that curled just enough to look wild.

A mouth made for sinning.

Eyes that promised danger.

He didn't smile when he noticed me.

He smirked.

Slow and cruel.

Loving A Monster

Like he already knew all the ways he would break me.

My heart hit the floor harder than my books did.

I dropped to my knees, gathering things in a panic.

I could feel him watching me.

I wished I could disappear into the floor.

Three

Maddox

She didn't belong here.

Not because she wasn't beautiful.

Because she didn't know she was.

A soft gray sweater hugged her curves in a way she probably hadn't meant to.

A black skirt brushed her knees.

Demure, sweet, the kind of thing that begged to be pushed up and ruined.

Her shoes were simple flats, not heels.

Loving A Monster

No makeup thick enough to hide the faint freckles dusting her nose.

She bent to pick up her books, skirt tugging higher on her thighs.

She flushed pink all the way to her ears.

I watched.

I smirked.

Everyone else pretended not to notice her.

I couldn't look away.

She was a siren wearing innocence like armor.

And I was already thinking about how good she'd look breaking under my hands.

Four

Dark Fascination

I saw the hunger in your stare.

The silent claim, the whispered dare.

You circled me with sharpened teeth.

A monster hiding underneath.

I bled my innocence like wine.

And still you whispered, "You are mine."

I didn't run. I didn't scream.

I walked into a monster's dream.

Five

Alianne

I felt it before I saw it.

A heat crawling up the back of my neck.

A shiver ran down my spine.

Someone was watching me.

I glanced up.

He hadn't moved.

Still leaning lazy and lethal against the far wall.

But now his gaze was pinned on me.

Alianne

Dark.

Heavy.

A slow, deliberate undressing.

My hands fumbled with my books again.

Clutching them tighter against my chest like a shield.

His mouth curved into a smile.

Not kind… Not friendly…

Something sharper.

Something that said, run.

And something that said, *stay and see what happens.*

Six

Maddox

She tried not to look.

She failed.

Her eyes darted back to me.

Wide and uncertain.

Her lip caught between her teeth in a nervous bite.

I pushed off the wall, slow, deliberate.

I crossed the room like I had all the time in the world.

Like she was the only thing worth wasting it on.

Maddox

She tensed when I stopped in front of her.

Good.

Seven

Maddox

"Careful, little lamb," I said, my voice low and lazy. "This place eats the soft ones alive."

She blinked up at me, lips parted, too stunned to answer.

I felt my gaze drag slowly down her body.

From the nervous twitch of her fingers.

To the soft swell of her chest.

Rising with each panicked breath.

To the exposed skin of her thighs, peeking from under her skirt.

Maddox

I made sure she saw it.

I made sure she felt it.

"Or maybe," I added, stepping just close enough.

She had to tilt her head to keep looking at me.

"They just like to play with them first."

Eight

Alianne

I could feel him staring at me.

It dragged across my skin.

Slow and heavy.

Like a brand that I couldn't scrub off.

My fingers twisted the strap of my bag tighter.

My throat a locked cage.

His smirk deepened—lethal and devastating.

I bit my lip.

Alianne

Not to be sexy.

To keep the panic from slipping out.

His eyes darkened immediately.

Like I'd just handed him the match and begged him to set the fire.

I hated the way my body responded.

I hated him for seeing it.

I lifted my chin.

Just a fraction.

Just enough to pretend I wasn't drowning.

His gaze sharpened- a blade now.

He saw the spark I hadn't meant to show.

And he smiled like he was going to burn me alive for it.

Nine

Maddox

She bit her lip.

She glared at me.

She looked like she wanted to slap me.

Or maybe she wanted to cry.

Maybe she wanted to cry and slap me.

All tangled up in one beautiful, trembling package.

My cock stirred.

My patience evaporated.

Maddox

I needed to see what else she would do.

I needed to see what else I could make her do.

I wasn't going to fuck her today.

I wasn't even going to touch her- not yet.

But I was going to own her.

Slowly.

Completely.

Starting now.

I watched her retreat.

And I smiled.

The hunt had begun.

Ten

Alianne

College is supposed to be survival.

Books, exams, cheap coffee, worse mistakes.

Not battles.

Not monsters.

Not boys who smile like wolves.

And yet-

There you were,

bloodthirsty in a black leather jacket,

Alianne

ruining peace just by existing.

Eleven

Maddox

She thought she could walk past me.

Like the storm would respect the fence.

Like teeth wouldn't notice soft skin.

Like a starving man wouldn't notice honey.

Cute.

Twelve

Alianne

I told myself I was imagining it.

That the shadows at the edges of my vision were tricks of light.

That the prickle across my skin had nothing to do with him.

I told myself a lot of things.

But none of them explained why my heart started racing every time I opened a door.

Why my body recognized him before my eyes did.

Thirteen

Alianne

I felt him before I saw him.

A shift in the air.

A tension threading the hallway like barbed wire.

I tried to turn back.

Too late.

He stepped out from behind the lockers.

All sharp danger and controlled violence.

And he blocked my path with nothing but a look.

Alianne

His steps were slow.

Measured.

Each one stealing air from my lungs.

I backed away, heart pounding, hands clutching my books like they could shield me.

He kept coming.

Predatory patience wrapped in shadows.

My back hit a wall.

He didn't stop until he was close enough to steal my breath.

"What do you want?"

My voice cracked, shame flooding my cheeks.

"Why won't you leave me alone?"

Fourteen

Chase Me, Break Me

I felt you in the hollow breath.

The space between my life and death.

You chase me through abandoned halls.

A phantom hand against the walls.

I flee, but faster comes your tread.

A hunter stitching dreams with dread.

You'll catch me, chain me, break me whole.

And fuck the fight out of my soul.

Fifteen

Maddox

I smiled- slow, sharp, merciless.

"I want you," I said, voice a rough growl.

I leaned in closer, watching her tremble.

Breathing her fear like oxygen.

"I want to feel you squirm under me."

"I want to hear you whimper when I touch you."

"I want to make you forget how to say no."

Sixteen

Alianne

My breath hitched-

My body shaking from the force of wanting him and hating him all at once.

"I'm not that kind of girl," I whispered.

"I'm-"

I swallowed the shame and embarrassment.

"I'm a virgin."

Seventeen

Maddox

Virgin.

The word slammed into me harder than any punch I'd ever taken.

My blood went molten.

My control shattered into razor-edged hunger.

"Good," I rasped, voice breaking into something dangerous.

"You'll be mine first."

"You'll be mine only."

I braced a hand beside her head.

Caging her in with my body.

I let my mouth brush her ear, slow and taunting.

"You think you can run from the person who already owns you?"

I laughed- a dark, low, filthy sound.

"Little lamb," I whispered, "You've already been caught."

Eighteen

Alianne

I ran.

His laughter followed me down the hall.

Dark and amused.

Like he already knew I would never really get away.

"You're a creep!" I spat over my shoulder.

"I'm not going to sleep with you, you psychopath!"

I heard his chuckle- low and deadly…

Just before I turned the corner.

It sounded like a promise.

Nineteen

Maddox

She thought words could save her.

Cute.

I didn't chase her down the hallway.

I didn't need to.

I knew where she slept.

Twenty

Alianne

I locked the door.

I double-checked the windows.

I still couldn't sleep.

The night pressed heavy against the glass.

Thick and trembling with something I couldn't name.

I turned over—heart finally slowing—and there he was.

Standing in my room.

Shadow and danger and sin incarnate.

Twenty-One

Maddox

She gasped- hands flying up to shove me away.

I caught them easily, pinned them above her head with one hand.

I used the other to cup her jaw.

Forcing her to meet my gaze.

"Still think you don't want me?" I whispered against her lips.

She shook her head.

But when I kissed her, she opened her mouth for me like a prayer.

Twenty-Two

Alianne

His mouth dragged down my throat.

Lower.

Lower.

Until his fingers found the hem of my sleep gown.

Slow… Deliberate…

He slid the fabric up, inch by inch.

Baring my stomach, my ribs, the aching swell of my breasts.

Until the gown bunched uselessly around my collarbones.

Alianne

I whimpered.

He kissed the curve of my hip.

Like he had all the time in the world.

Twenty-Three

Maddox

I stared down at her.

All flushed skin and heaving chest.

Lips swollen from my kiss.

Innocence and surrender bleeding off her in waves.

My mouth watered.

I dragged my tongue up the inside of her thigh.

Slowly and punishingly, savoring the way she trembled.

I licked her like I had all night.

Maddox

Slow circles, teasing flicks.

Until her hips bucked helplessly against my mouth.

I didn't stop until she shattered.

Crying out my name in the dark.

Wet and broken and mine.

I pulled her gown back down, covering her shaking body.

"You're coming to the party Friday," I said, my voice soft and lethal.

She shook her head weakly, eyes glassy.

I smiled against her neck.

"Or I tell everyone, how sweet you tasted when you came on my tongue."

Twenty-Four

Alianne

I told myself I could do this.

Walk in, blend into the noise, and pretend he didn't exist.

The music thudded through the floorboards.

Bodies swayed, laughed, and drank.

A writhing, sweaty mass of forgetfulness.

I kept my head down.

I didn't look for him.

I didn't let myself feel the burn of his gaze.

Alianne

Heavy relentless from across the room.

Twenty-Five

Maddox

She thought she could ignore me.

Cute.

I leaned against the wall, arms crossed.

Watching her weave through the crowd like a lost lamb.

She was beautiful tonight.

Dress riding high on trembling thighs.

The tight material stretched over soft curves.

A good girl dropped into a wolf's den.

Maddox

I let her pretend for a while.

I liked watching her squirm.

Twenty-Six

Alianne

He wasn't the one I should have been afraid of.

It was the boy in the kitchen.

Beer breath and clumsy hands.

Laughter too loud, touching too much.

"Dance with me," he slurred, grabbing my wrist.

I tried to pull away.

That's when the room cracked apart.

Twenty-Seven

Maddox

I was on him before he could blink.

One punch—blood sprayed against the wall.

The boy crumpled, groaning.

I stepped over him, breathing hard, rage blistering under my skin.

"Back the fuck off," I snarled at the crowd.

"She's mine."

Twenty-Eight

Alianne

Everyone stared.

At him.

At me.

I wanted to disappear.

My cheeks burned.

My eyes blurred.

I turned and fled-

Upstairs, down halls, past doors swinging open and shut.

Alianne

Until I found an empty hallway and leaned against the wall, gasping for air.

Twenty-Nine

Maddox

I followed her.

Silent.

Relentless.

I caught her wrist before she could bolt again.

Spun her into a dark room, kicked the door shut.

Her back hit the wall.

I caged her in with my body.

Hands flat against the wood beside her head.

Maddox

"You're not running from me," I growled, voice low and feral.

"Not anymore."

Thirty

Maddox

I slammed the door behind us.

Good.

I needed her scared.

I needed her trembling.

I needed her to understand she belonged to me.

"You dressed up," I snarled, voice low and vicious.

"You ignored me."

"You made that little fucker think he could touch you."

Maddox

I leaned closer, my hands braced beside her head.

"It's your fault he got hit."

Thirty-One

Alianne

It's not my fault you're violent!" I snapped, heart hammering against my ribs.

"It's not my fault you can't leave me alone!"

I shoved at his chest, but he didn't move.

He smiled—slow, dark, devastating.

"Then tell me," he whispered, his voice like velvet over a blade.

"Who were you trying to impress dressed like that?"

Thirty-Two

Maddox

She shook her head.

"No one," she whispered.

Liar.

I slid my hand down the front of her dress-

Palming her breast roughly through the fabric, kneading it until she whimpered.

Her nipples pebbled against my hand, aching and desperate.

I smiled against her throat.

Then dragged my hand lower,

Loving A Monster

Lifting the hem of her dress with brutal patience.

Thirty-Three

Alianne

His fingers shoved between my thighs.

Without hesitation, without mercy.

Two thick fingers sliding inside me,

Stretching me, filling me in a way that stole the breath from my lungs.

I gasped. Loud… broken… back arching against the door.

Nails scraping helplessly down his arm.

My body betrayed me… again…

My hips rolled against his hand.

Loving A Monster

Desperate, frantic…

Chasing the pleasure he was dragging out of me.

Thirty-Four

Maddox

I felt her tighten around my fingers.

I felt the tremble start in her thighs.

She was close.

I pulled my fingers out and sucked her juices off my fingers.

She whined- a high, broken sound that made my cock throb against my jeans.

I pressed my fingers against her lips.

"Not tonight," I said, my voice like gravel and smoke.

"Tonight's about me."

Thirty-Five

Maddox

I pulled her down by her hair- gentle but unrelenting.

"On your knees, little lamb."

She resisted for half a heartbeat.

The crumbled, sinking down onto the carpet at my feet.

Dress bunched around her thighs, cheeks burning with humiliation and heat.

I unzipped my jeans, pulling my cock free—already hard and aching for her.

I fisted her hair, tilting her face up to me.

Maddox

"Look at you," I rasped, my voice shredded with lust.

"So pretty on your knees where you belong."

Her mouth opened slowly.

Hesitant… Ashamed… Aching…

I brushed the leaking tip of my cock against her lips.

Painting her mouth with my hunger.

Savoring the way her cheeks flushed hotter.

Thirty-Six

Alianne

He slid between my lips—slow, teasing, filthy.

His groan rumbled deep in his chest.

Dark satisfaction wrapped in something rawer, something terrifying.

I hollowed my cheeks like he'd told me.

Wrapped my lips tight around him.

Trying to ignore the taste of salt and sin filling my mouth.

Thirty-Seven

Maddox

"Good girl," I grunted, hand tightening in her hair.

"Such a good little mouth."

"Suck me like you mean it, lamb."

She whimpered. The vibrations shooting straight through my cock.

Making my control slip another notch.

I couldn't hold back.

I thrust into her mouth, slowly at first, letting her adjust.

The deeper, harder, crueler.

She gagged around me, hands flying up to brace against my thighs.

Nails digging into my jeans.

I didn't stop.

I fucked her mouth like it was mine to destroy.

Because it was.

Because she was.

Thirty-Eight

Alianne

I tried to breath through my nose.

Tried to stay still… Tried not to choke…

But he was relentless. Using my mouth like it belonged to him.

Tears burned down my cheeks.

My throat ached.

My knees shook.

And still I stayed.

Because some sick, broken part of me needed to be used by him.

Thirty-Nine

Maddox

I felt her surrender.

The moment her body stopped fighting and started offering itself up instead.

I growled low in my chest, hips snapping harder, faster.

"Take it," I snarled, breath ragged.

"Take all of me, little lamb."

"Swallow every fucking drop."

My orgasm ripped through me—brutal, shattering.

And I held her there, buried deep.

Maddox

Spilling down her throat until she gagged and whimpered against me.

Forty

Alianne

He pulled out slowly.

Dragging every inch over my raw, swollen lips.

I collapsed against the wall, coughing, wiping my mouth with the back of my hand.

He crouched in front of me, smirking like the devil he was.

"That's my good girl," he whispered, his voice wicked and proud.

Forty-One

Maddox

I knelt down in front of her.

Heart pounding in my throat like a fucking drum.

Her lips were red and swollen.

Her cheeks were tear-streaked.

She looked so beautiful.

She looked like something I would die for.

I wiped the corner of her mouth with my thumb.

Slow… Careful… Reverent.

Loving A Monster

Her breath hitched.

I tangled my fingers in her hair.

Not to control.

But to soothe.

"Mine," I whispered.

Not a threat.

Not a warning.

Just a raw, broken truth.

Forty-Two

Alianne

He touched me like I was something fragile.

He looked at me like I was something he was scared he'd already broken,

I didn't understand it.

I hated how much it made my chest ache.

I hated that some twisted part of me enjoyed this.

Wanted to lean into him.

Wanted to be his.

Forty-Three

Alianne

He pulled me to my feet.

His touch almost gentle.

A ghost brushing against bruises he didn't even know he left.

For a second. Just one aching second.

I believed there might be something real hiding under all the darkness.

I believed him.

We pushed open the door.

The party roared around us—music, laughter, chaos.

Alianne

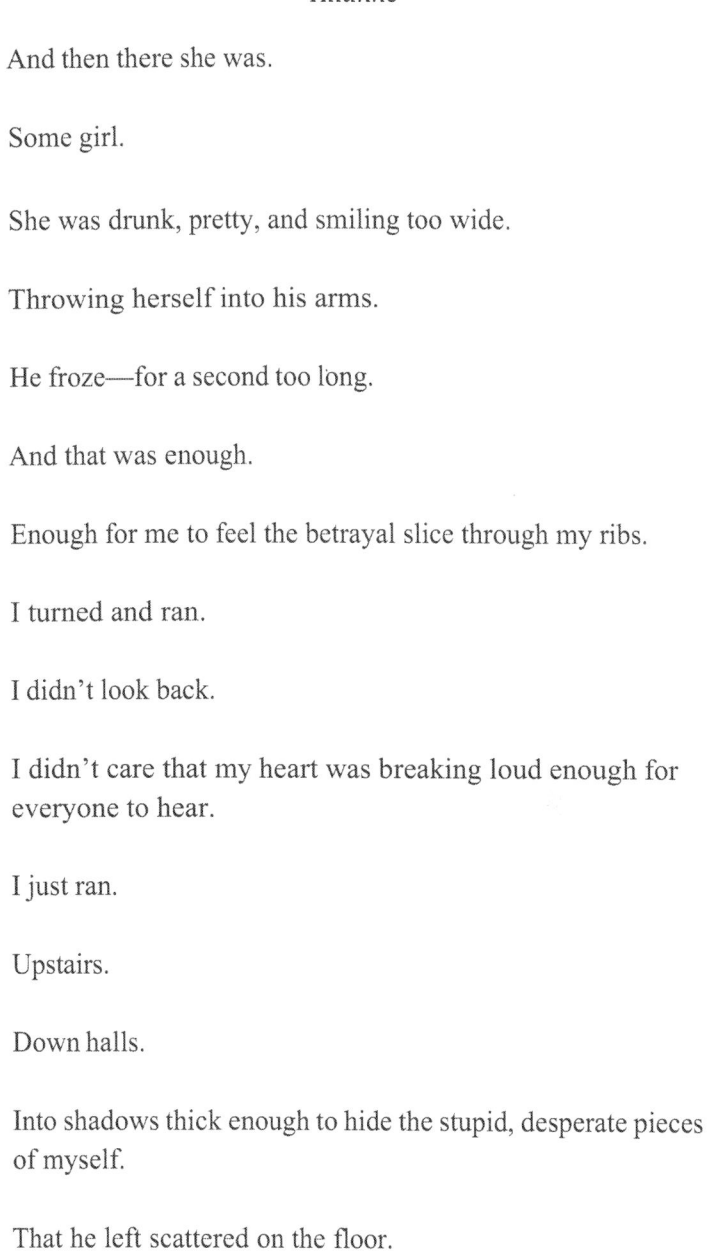

And then there she was.

Some girl.

She was drunk, pretty, and smiling too wide.

Throwing herself into his arms.

He froze—for a second too long.

And that was enough.

Enough for me to feel the betrayal slice through my ribs.

I turned and ran.

I didn't look back.

I didn't care that my heart was breaking loud enough for everyone to hear.

I just ran.

Upstairs.

Down halls.

Into shadows thick enough to hide the stupid, desperate pieces of myself.

That he left scattered on the floor.

Forty-Four

Maddox

I shoved the girl off me—-not gently.

My eyes were already tracking her.

My girl, disappearing into the dark like a wound I hadn't stitched fast enough.

Rage boiled inside of me. She thought she could run from me.

She thought she could hide.

She forgot who owned her.

Forty-Five

Alianne

I ducked into a spare room, breath coming in broken gasps.

I locked the door.

I pressed my back against it, heart screaming in my chest.

I needed space.

I needed to get him out of my head.

I needed…

Forty-Six

Maddox

I found the first door locked.

I smiled.

She was scared.

She was trying to hide.

Good.

It would make catching her even sweeter.

Forty-Seven

Alianne

I heard the doorknob rattle.

My breath caught in my throat.

"Alianne," his voice purred through the crack.

Low… Dark… Terrifying… Seductive…

"Come out, little lamb."

"Let's play."

He rattled the doorknob again. Harder this time.

My hands scrambled against the window latch.

Loving A Monster

Heart battering my ribs like a trapped bird.

I shoved the window open and climbed out.

Dress catching on the sill.

Palms scraping against the rough brick.

Lungs heaving with terror and something worse:

Hope.

Forty-Eight

Alianne

The trees closed around me.

Dark and wild, whispering secrets to the night.

I stumbled, branches slapping against my skin.

Roots clawing at my ankles.

I didn't know where I was going.

I just knew he was behind me.

I could feel him.

In the air… in my blood.

Loving A Monster

The faster I ran.

The harder my body ached for him to catch me.

Forty-Nine

Maddox

I let her think she could escape.

I let her run herself ragged.

I let her get just far enough to feel hope.

Then I lunged.

Dragging her down into the dirt.

Pinning her with my weight.

Her breath punched out in a sharp gasp.

I rolled her onto her back, straddling her hips.

Trapping her under me.

"Tired yet, little lamb?" I rasped, voice shredded with hunger.

Fifty

Alianne

I should have screamed.

I should have fought.

Instead I spread my legs wider.

Letting him settle deeper between them.

My dress was already ruined, bunched around my waist.

Torn by branches and desperation.

"Please," I gasped.

Not for mercy.

Loving A Monster

For more.

Fifty-One

Maddox

I didn't undress her carefully.

I didn't kiss her softly.

I shoved her panties aside with brutal fingers.

Lining myself up against her slick, trembling entrance.

"You want it rough, little lamb?" I growled.

Dragging the fat head of my cock through her soaked folds.

"You want to be fucked like a whore?"

"My whore."

Fifty-Two

Alianne

~~~

"Yes, I gasped-

Raw, wrecked, and desperate.

"Please, Maddox."

Fifty-Three

Maddox

I slammed into her in one savage thrust.

Tearing past the resistance of her virgin body.

Burying myself to the hilt inside her heat.

She cried out—my name on her lips.

I stilled, shaking with the effort it took not to lose it completely.

"Mine," I snarled against her throat.

Teeth scraping skin.

Hands bruising hips.

Loving A Monster

"Fucking mine."

I fucked her like I needed it to breathe.

Her nails raked my back.

Her cries spilling into the wild night.

I grabbed her throat—not to hurt, just to hold her still.

As I drove into her again and again and again.

Fifty-Four

Claimed in Dirt and Sky

You chased me through the breaking trees.

Your hunger ripping through the leaves.

You caught me gasping, gashed, and bare.

Shoved my face into the air.

Your hand was rough against my throat.

Your cock so deep inside my coat.

You fucked me hard into the mud.

You made me beg, you made me flood.

Loving A Monster

You kissed my spine, my wrists, and my cries.

You stripped the stars out from the skies.

I broke for you—I bled, I burned.

Fifty-Five

Alianne

I shattered.

My body locking up around him.

Pulse screaming in my ears.

Pleasure ripping through me so violently. I thought I might die from it.

And still he didn't stop.

He fucked me through it.

He fucked me until my vision blurred and my voice broke and my soul gave up fighting.

Fifty-Six

Maddox

I came with a roar. Deep inside her.

Filling her with every brutal, broken piece of myself.

I collapsed over her, panting, heart battering against hers.

She didn't protest when I lifted her into my arms.

Her body limp against mine—wrecked, tender, beautiful.

I held her close, my jacket wrapped around her battered skin.

Fury still simmering in my veins—not at her.

At the world that would dare to bruise what was mine.

Fifty-Seven

Alianne

I barely remember the drive.

Just the steady thud of his heart against my ear.

His jacket wrapped around me.

Too big, too warm, smelling like leather, smelling like him.

His hand in my hair.

Stroking slow, thoughtless patterns in my hair like he didn't even realize he was doing it.

And for reasons I couldn't name.

I let him hold me.

Fifty-Eight

Alianne

I woke up to the pale gray light of the morning.

Tangled in unfamiliar sheets.

Sore and aching in places I didn't even know I had.

His arm was heavy around my waist.

Anchoring me to the bed, to him.

I held my breath.

Slowly peeling his arm off.

Inching out from under him.

Alianne

Feet finding the floor like I was walking a minefield.

I made it three steps before his voice stopped me cold.

Fifty-Nine

Maddox

"Where do you think you're going, little lamb?"

My voice was a growl, still rough from sleep… Or maybe just rage.

I was already out of bed, stalking toward her.

Naked, half-hard, hungry for her.

She froze.

Trembling.

Beautiful.

Guilt written all over her face.

Maddox

I grabbed her by her hair.

Not cruel, but firmly enough to make her gasp.

I pushed her down to her knees at the edge of the bed.

"You don't get to run from me," I growled, fisting my cock in my hand.

"You want to act like a bad girl?"

"You get treated like one."

Sixty

Alianne

His cock brushed my lips.

Thick, heavy, and already leaking.

I opened for him—part protest, part addiction, letting his slide inside.

He set the rhythm.

Shallow thrusts at first.

Slow and punishing.

Filling my mouth until my jaw ached and my throat burned.

Sixty-One

Maddox

It wasn't enough.

I needed more.

I pulled her up onto the bed.

Flipping her onto her back.

Dragging her hips towards my mouth.

I lowered myself onto her.

Mouth on her cunt.

Cock pressing against her lips from above.

Sixty-Two

Alianne

His tongue was relentless.

Sliding through my folds.

Flicking over my clit until my thighs trembled around his head.

I moaned around his cock.

Drool slipping from the corners of my mouth.

Unable to stop sucking even as pleasure ripped through me.

Sixty-Three

Maddox

She tasted like sin and surrender.

Sweet and filthy and mine.

I sucked her clit between my lips.

Shoving two fingers inside her dripping pussy.

Thrusting them hard enough to make her entire body shake beneath me.

Her throat vibrated around my cock with every cry.

I groaned against her.

Lost… Ruined… Home…

Sixty-Four

Alianne

I came against his mouth.

Hips jerking, sobbing broken sounds around his cock.

Shattering into white-hot pieces I couldn't put back together.

Sixty-Five

Maddox

I pulled out of her mouth just in time.

Stroking myself once, twice…

Spilling across her pretty, ruined face with a growl.

Marking her.

Branding her.

Mine.

Forever.

Sixty-Six

Tangled in Filth and Worship

Your mouth drowned me, wild and sweet.

My cunt spread raw beneath your teeth.

I sucked you slow; I sucked you deep.

Your cock, my prayer between my cheeks.

You fucked my mouth with ruthless need.

I licked your slit; I drank your greed.

My thighs shook wide, your tongue drove in.

Your fingers coaxed a quake from skin.

Tangled in Filth and Worship

I swallowed every brutal moan.

You tongued the shudder from my bones.

We broke together, mouth and spit.

No heaven left that we don't split.

Sixty-Seven

Maddox

She was a wreck.

Bruised, sore, and shaking from the weight of what we'd done.

I ran a bath, hot and steaming.

The scent of soap and sweat and surrender curling into the air.

I lifted her into the water.

Slow... Careful... my hands rough and reverent all at once.

I should have let her soak.

I should have let her breathe.

Maddox

Instead, I slid into the tub behind her.

Spreading her thighs over my lap.

Feeling the heat of her against my cock.

Feeling the way her body tensed and melted at the same time.

Sixty-Eight

Alianne

His cock pressed against my entrance.

Still tender, still aching-

But I didn't fight.

I tilted my hips back, offering myself to him.

Needing him as much as I hated him.

Sixty-Nine

Maddox

I drove into her.

Slow at first.

Groaning at the way she stretched around me.

Still so tight.

So perfect.

So fucking mine.

The water sloshed over the edge of the tub with every brutal thrust.

Her gasps echoed off the tiled walls.

Loving A Monster

Sweet, broken, desperate.

Seventy

Maddox

She came with a broken sob.

Clenching around me.

Trembling in my arms like a shattered prayer.

I stayed inside her until her body sagged against mine.

Limp… Ruined… Beautiful…

Then I pulled out.

Kissed the back of her neck.

And left her there.

Soaking in the tub.

Full of me.

Seventy-One

Maddox

She stared out the window.

Silent... Flushed... and still wearing my shirt.

I didn't care if the whole world saw her in my clothes.

I wanted them to know she was mine.

I parked outside her apartment, engine still rumbling low under us.

Seventy-Two

Maddox

"You're mine," I said.

Not a question.

Not a plea.

A decree.

Seventy-Three

Alianne

I turned to him-

Heart pounding, mouth dry.

"I'm not yours," I whispered.

Even though my body screamed the lie.

Seventy-Four

Maddox

I grabbed her throat.

Not enough to hurt.

But enough to make her breath catch.

Enough to pin her against the passenger seat with no escape.

My face was inches from hers-

Eyes dark, lips curled in a slow, savage smile.

Seventy-Five

Maddox

"You're mine," I whispered against her mouth.

"You have been since the moment I laid eyes on you."

"You always will be mine."

She gasped, hips arching helplessly, thighs clenching.

I loosened my grip.

Kissed her forehead like a twisted benediction.

Pulled back just enough to watch her pant and shake under me.

"You were saying?"

Seventy-Six

Alianne

I got dressed for class like nothing had changed.

Jeans.

Hoodie.

Hair thrown into a messy knot like I wasn't unraveling inside.

I walked to campus with my head down.

Counting cracks in the sidewalk.

Pretending the bruises on my hips didn't exist.

Pretending I wasn't full of him still.

Seventy-Seven

Alianne

I slid into the back corner.

Safe, invisible, forgotten.

Until he sat down beside me.

Maddox.

Smirking.

Sprawled out like he owned the room.

Like he owned me.

His knees brushed mine under the desk-

Deliberate.

Possessive.

I froze.

He smiled wider.

Seventy-Eight

Maddox

She looked like she wanted to sink into the floor.

I didn't care.

She was mine.

And the world was going to learn it.

Class by class.

Breath by breath

Bruise by bruise.

Seventy-Nine

Alianne

He showed up everywhere.

Sitting beside me in every lecture.

Leaning against the class door when I tried to slip away unnoticed.

Waiting outside my form like a shadow stitched to my heels

Eighty

Maddox

I brushed her hair off her neck between classes.

Exposed the bruises I'd left there.

Kissed the hollow of her throat like a brand.

She shivered.

So did I.

Eighty-One

Alianne

People stared.

Whispers followed me down the halls.

Why is he with her?

What did she do to get Maddox Cross attention?

I wanted to scream.

I wanted to disappear.

I wanted to hate him.

But every time his hand found the small of my back.

Alianne

Every time his fingers slid possessively around my wrists.

Every time his mouth brushed my ear with dark promises.

My body betrays me all over again.

Eighty-Two

Alianne

It had been two days.

Two whole days without him glued to my side.

I told myself I was relieved.

I told myself I was free.

I almost believed it.

I went to the coffee shop off campus.

Books spread out.

Earbuds in.

Alianne

Pretending I was just another girl living a normal life.

Eighty-Three

Alianne

I didn't notice him until he was standing awkwardly at my table.

The boy from the party.

His hand scratched the back of his neck.

His face flushed with shame.

"Hey," he said, his voice low.

"I'm sorry about that night; I was drunk, and I shouldn't have grabbed you.

I nodded stiffly.

Alianne

Wanting the conversation over before it even began.

Eighty-Four

Maddox

I spotted her through the glass.

Head bent over books, sweater sliding off one shoulder.

So fucking sweet, and soft and mine.

And then I saw him.

Standing too close.

Talking too much.

Her mouth pressed into a tight, miserable line.

Eighty-Five

Maddox

I pushed the door open.

The bell above the door rang like a death knell.

I didn't run.

I didn't shout.

I stalked—slow, patient, inevitable—across the room.

Never taking my eyes off her.

Eighty-Six

Alianne

Maddox slid into the chair beside me like he belonged there.

Body coiled tight.

Eyes burning through the boy still stupidly trying to talk to me.

He didn't say anything.

He didn't have to.

The boy stammered something about leaving.

Tripping over himself as he backed away from the table and fled into the cold morning.

Eighty-Seven

Maddox

I leaved over-

Nose brushing her hair.

Voice a rasp of steel and smoke.

"You don't talk to other men," I said, soft, brutal, and final.

"You're mine, little lamb."

"Only mine."

Eighty-Eight

Alianne

I stopped pretending.

Somewhere between his mouth and his hands.

The way he says *mine* like a vow-

I stopped pretending I didn't want it.

I stopped pretending I didn't want *him.*

Eighty-Nine

Maddox

She didn't think I noticed.

The way her breath hitched when I chased her down the empty hallways at night.

The way her thighs pressed together when I growled into her ear.

She liked it.

She liked running.

She liked being caught.

Ninety

Maddox

I gave chase.

Always.

I let her feel the thrill of it.

Her blood racing.

Her heart hammering.

Then I caught her.

Every time.

Ninety-One

Alianne

I ran.

Every time.

I let him hunt me down.

Let him pin me against lockers.

Let him fuck the fear and fight out of me.

Until there was nothing left but pleasure and surrender.

And I loved it.

I loved every ruined, broken second.

Ninety-Two

Alianne

I smiled at someone.

A boy I didn't even know.

I didn't mean anything by it.

I didn't even realize Maddox had seen.

Not until he grabbed my wrist and dragged me down the hall.

Ninety-Three

The Price of Smiling

I smiled too sweet, I looked too long.

And now you write me into wrong.

Hands at my throat, hips at my back.

You punish every breath I lack.

My legs shake, and my skin turns red.

I pay the price inside your bed.

Ninety-Four

Maddox

I didn't say a word.

I kicked open the bathroom door.

Pushed her inside.

Locked it behind us.

I spun her around to face the mirror.

Hands braced against the sink.

Shoving her dress above her hips.

"You think you can flirt, little lamb?"

Maddox

"You think you can fucking smile at someone else?"

Ninety-Five

Alianne

His hands fisted my hair, yanking me head back so I could see.

See my flushed face.

See my swollen lips.

See the filthy, desperate way I arched my back into him.

His cock slid between my thighs.

Thick and demanding.

And he didn't wait for permission.

Ninety-Six

Maddox

I fucked her against the sink.

Brutal and punishing.

Hips slamming into her.

Hand muffled over her mouth to muffle her cries.

"Mine, " I growled.

"Mine."

"Fucking mine!"

Ninety-Seven

Alianne

I shattered-

Body breaking against the porcelain.

Gasping, sobbing, burning alive in his hands.

I hated him.

I loved him.

I would never survive him.

Ninety-Eight

Alianne

It started small.

A flower tucked into my locker.

A note slipped under my door.

You looked beautiful today.

You belong to me.

I'll always find you.

I'm always watching.

Ninety-Nine

Wrong Hands, Wrong Love

Love rotted in the wrong man's hands.

Built on broken, bleeding plans.

Roses wilt, and gifts decay.

A poisoned love that stalks its prey.

He smiled while slipping in the knife.

Calling it care, calling it life.

One Hundred

Alianne

I was looking for him, through the crowded house of party-goers.

I found him.

And her.

That same girl.

Throwing herself into his arms.

Pressing her mouth against his in front of everyone.

I ran.

Again.

Loving A Monster

Because I was stupid enough to believe he was different.

Because I was stupid enough to think monsters could love.

One Hundred and One

Alianne

I heard footsteps behind me-

Fast… Deliberate… Heavy

"Maddox," I gasped.

Half hope, half terror.

But it wasn't him.-

One Hundred and Two

Alianne

A hand grabbed my arm.

Another clamped over my mouth.

I kicked, clawed, and bit.

But the world tilted sideways.

Stars exploding behind my eyes.

Everything went black.

One Hundred and Three

Bleed Me, Leave Me

You bled me slow with lips and lies.

A kiss beneath a stranger's eyes.

I ran into the wolf's wide grin.

A door unlocked, a darkness pinned.

If love is loss, then lose me quick.

If trust is death, then make me sick.

One Hundred and Four

Alianne

Cold concrete.

The smell of mildew and sweat.

My wrists were chained to the wall.

He sat across from me.

Smiling like this was a date.

Twirling a knife between his fingers.

"You made Maddox Cross punch me in front of everyone," he said, his voice furious and sweet.

"You made him want you."

Alianne

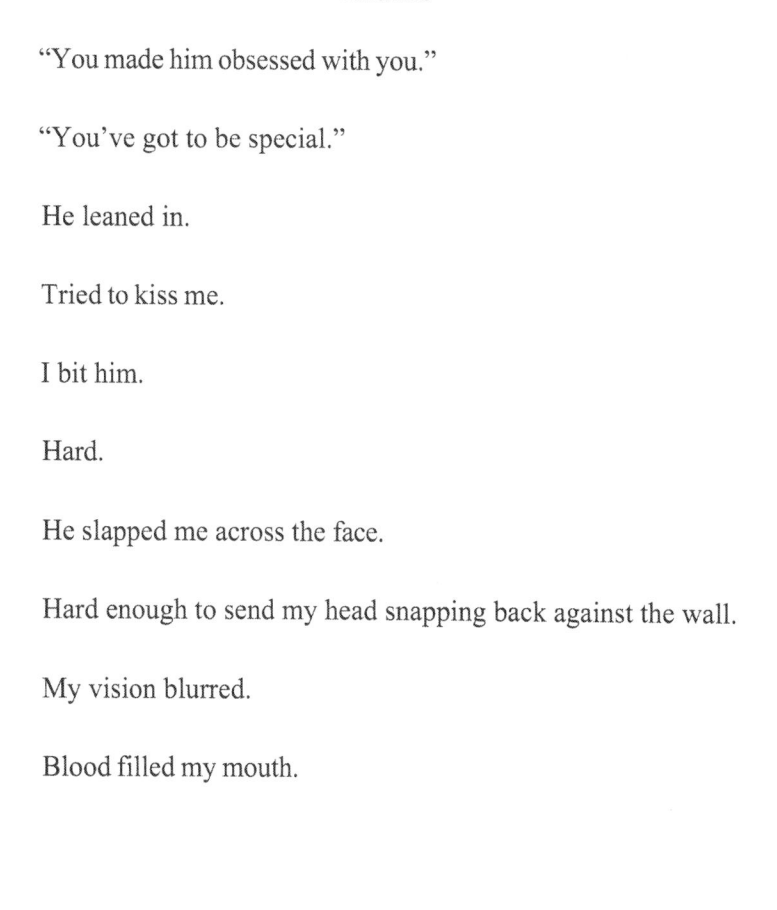

"You made him obsessed with you."

"You've got to be special."

He leaned in.

Tried to kiss me.

I bit him.

Hard.

He slapped me across the face.

Hard enough to send my head snapping back against the wall.

My vision blurred.

Blood filled my mouth.

One Hundred and Five

Maddox

She was gone.

She hadn't answered her phone.

She hadn't been seen leaving the party.

I found her phone smashed in the woods.

The world went red.

I was going to kill whoever touched her.

No one could take what belonged to me.

One Hundred and Six

Maddox

Two days.

Two fucking days without a trace of her.

Every breath felt like swallowing broken shards of glass.

Every heartbeat felt like bleeding out one more second without her.

She was gone.

Vanished.

My little lamb—stolen from me.

One Hundred and Seven

Maddox

I almost broke the door off its hinges when the knock came.

And there she was.

The girl from the party.

The one who kissed me.

Pale.

Shaking.

Crying.

"I didn't know he'd actually hurt her!"

Maddox

"It was just supposed to scare her!"

"But he—he took her."

"My brother…"

"There's an old shack in the woods-

Near the south ridge.

"We found it a month or so ago."

I didn't want to hear the rest.

I was already moving.

I was going to bring her home.

And I was going to kill him for touching what was mine.

One Hundred and Eight

Maddox

The shack crouched at the edge of the clearing.

Half collapsed, swallowed by creeping vines and wild grass.

The roof sagged in the middle.

Black mold creeping like rot along the wooden slats.

A single window.

Cracked, dirty, and covered in grime so thick.

It looked like a cataract staring blindly into the woods.

I didn't hesitate.

Maddox

I kicked the door open and tore the world apart.

One Hundred and Nine

Maddox

She was sprawled on the floor.

Wrists bound.

Head lolled to one side.

Unconscious.

And him- the worthless fucking coward.

Straddling her hips.

His pants shoved halfway down his thighs.

His cock out.

Maddox

One hand fisting himself.

The other clawing, fumbling.

Trying and failing to shove her dress up.

Her body didn't move.

Not even when he grunted and cursed.

Hands shaking in frustration.

That was the last thing he would ever do.

I was on him before he could look up.

I ripped him off of her.

Slammed him into the wall so hard the boards cracked like brittle bones.

He screamed.

I didn't hear it.

My fists found his face.

One.

Two.

Loving A Monster

Three.

Each blow harder than the last.

Shattering bone.

Spraying teeth and blood across the floor.

He tried to beg.

I crushed his throat with one brutal punch.

Watched the light leave his eyes.

Only then.

Only when there was nothing left but ruin at my feet.

Did I turn back to her.

One Hundred and Ten

Maddox

She was too still.

Too quiet.

My hands shook as I cut the bindings from her wrists.

Scooped her broken, sacred body into my arms.

"Got you," I whispered.

Mouth against her forehead.

"You're safe, little lamb."

One Hundred and Eleven

Maddox

I carried her gently into my apartment.

Laid her on the bed.

Stripped the ruined dress from her body with hands that shook.

Harder than they ever had in a fight.

I found a washcloth.

Warm water, soap.

And I cleaned the blood and dirt from her skin.

Every bruise I uncovered felt like a knife to my chest.

Maddox

I kissed the inside of her wrist where the chains had marred her perfect skin.

"I'm sorry," I murmured, voice wrecked and hollow.

I dropped my forehead to her bare thigh.

Breathing her in.

Begging for forgiveness without saying the words.

"The girl—the one you saw kissing me—she's the sister of the fucker who took you.

"They set it up."

"He wanted to make you run so he could have you."

I lifted my head.

Met her wide, wet eyes.

Saw the way her mouth trembled.

"I never wanted her."

"I only want you."

"It was always you, little lamb."

One Hundred and Twelve

A Vow Written in Blood

I found you bruised beneath the sky,

A broken breath, a hollow cry.

I took an oath with blood and bone:

You'll never break. You'll never be alone.

I'll tear the stars; I'll drown the flood.

I love you best when soaked in blood.

One Hundred and Thirteen

Alianne

His words hit harder than his fists ever could.

I saw it.

The devastation on his face.

The blood still under his nails.

The desperate way he held me again.

Like he thought I might vanish again.

He would have died for me.

He had killed for me.

Loving A Monster

I reached for him.

Fingers threading into his messy hair.

Pulling his mouth down to mine.

It wasn't gentle.

It was desperate.

One Hundred and Fourteen

Maddox

I lifted her.

Cradling her weight against me.

Lowering her onto the bed with a gentleness that hurt worse than any violation.

I spread her thighs with shaking hands.

"Mine," I whispered.

"Always mine."

When I slid inside her.

It wasn't to punish, or to mark, or to break.

Loving A Monster

It was to belong.

One Hundred and Fifteen

Alianne

He moved slow-

Deep thrusts, heavy and aching,

Like he was trying to memorize the way I wrapped around him.

I clung to him.

Nails digging into his back.

Mouth gasping against his throat.

One Hundred and Sixteen

Worship the Wreckage

Kiss my wounds, and I'll kiss yours.

Stitch my soul behind locked doors.

Love the cracks, the shattered bends.

Worship what the fire sends.

I'll heal the wreckage, rise in flame.

I'll answer only to your name.

One Hundred and Seventeen

Maddox

She was so tight, so warm, so damn alive.

It nearly undid me.

I buried my face in her hair.

Breathing her in like salvation.

I moved slower than I ever had.

Grinding into her.

Pulling her cries into my mouth.

Making love to her like she was the last thing I'd ever touch.

One Hundred and Eighteen

Alianne

I came apart around him.

Body locking up.

Tears spilling down my cheeks.

He held me through it.

Fucking me through it.

Until I couldn't tell where he ended and I began.

And when the words ripped out of me.

They came out like a sob and a promise all at once.

One Hundred and Nineteen

Maddox

I came with a roar.

Burying myself deep inside her.

Marking her forever.

One Hundred and Twenty

No God But You

I never prayed until I knelt.

Beneath the hand your hunger dealt.

No altar high, no sinner's view.

I found my heaven in your hands.

I found my death in your demands.

One Hundred and Twenty-One

Maddox

We stayed like that-

bruised, bloody, whole.

But together.

Against the world.

Against everything.

Made in the USA
Columbia, SC
30 April 2025